Mousey Mousey

Featherbrain

Ginger stripes

Stripey tabby

Mischief

Half Pint

Mackerel and White

Ginger and White

Kitten Tales

For Yvonne Streatfield
S.G.

For Steve, with love
K.S.

ORCHARD BOOKS
96 Leonard Street, London EC2A 4RH
Orchard Books Australia
14 Mars Road, Lane Cove, NSW 2066
Text © Sally Grindley 1997
Illustrations © Kate Simpson 1997
First published in Great Britain 1997
The right of Sally Grindley to be identified as the Author and
Kate Simpson as the Illustrator of this Work has been asserted by them
in accordance with the Copyright, Designs and Patents Act, 1988.
A CIP catalogue record for this book is available from the British Library.
1 85213 995 1
Printed in Malaysia

Kitten Tales

Sally Grindley

Illustrated by Kate Simpson

ORCHARD BOOKS

Cont

Mumcat 10

Mischief 18

Half Pint 26

Bulldozer 35

YumYum 44

ents

Mumcat

Mumcat was feeling very pleased with herself. Mumcat was *looking* very pleased with herself. The grin on her face spread her whiskers from ear to ear. "Meow," she said gently, because she wanted to.

Mumcat

Mumcat lay in the garden shed where an old feather cushion had been thrown. It was warm and dark and safe in the corner. No one knew she was there, but she wasn't lonely, not a bit. Mumcat had just become a mum. Beneath her tum seven tiny sausage-shaped kittens wriggled and nuzzled and fed from her milk.

Seven kittens! None of her friends had seven kittens. Three? Yes. Four? Yes. Five? Yes. Even six. But seven? Seven was a lot.

Kitten Tales

Seven little mouths to feed. That was a lot of feeding. Seven little bodies to lick clean. That was a lot of licking. Seven names to find. That was a lot of names.

The trouble with the feeding was that seven little kittens wanted to feed at the same time. They pushed, they trod on each other, they even sat on each other.

The trouble
with the
licking clean was
that seven little
kittens fidgeted,
rolled around,
crawled away, and
made her tongue very tired.

The trouble with choosing the names was that she didn't know what to choose. She knew a few names, like Tiddles, Sooty, Fluff, Tom, Kitty and Ginger, but they were other cats' names for other kittens. Her kittens were special to her, and she wanted names that would be special to them.

"I'll wait and I'll watch and as they grow older I'll know what to call them," Mumcat thought to herself. So she waited and she watched and one by one the names came.

Kitten Tales

One little kitten tore a hole in the feather cushion and feathers flew everywhere. He spent a whole hour running around with a feather sticking to the top of his head.

"You're my Featherbrain!" said Mumcat.

Another little kitten never stopped eating. She would try anything, even paper, and spiders, and sand, and leaves.

"You're my Yum Yum!" said Mumcat.

A third little kitten
never stopped boasting
that she would catch a mouse.
"You're my Mousey Mousey!"
said Mumcat.

A fourth little kitten was
always getting into trouble,
and knocking things over.
"You're my Bulldozer!"
said Mumcat.

Kitten Tales

A fifth little kitten always wanted to know what was going on and was always first to find something new.
"You're my Peebo!" said Mumcat.

A sixth little kitten was just plain naughty.
"You're my Mischief!" said Mumcat.

Mumcat's seventh little kitten was
only half the size of the others and
always seemed to miss out at food time.
"You're my Half Pint!" said Mumcat.
Seven little kittens, and one very proud
Mumcat.

Mischief

There were woods behind the house where the kittens lived. Mumcat said, "Whatever you do, don't go into the woods behind the house, not until you are older. You might get frightened. You might get lost. There are foxes there."

The kittens often peered into the woods behind the house from the safety of the garden. It looked an exciting place to be. They could have adventures there. They could climb trees there. They could play hide-and-seek there. But Mumcat had said, "Whatever you do, don't go into the woods behind the house."

Featherbrain, Yum Yum, Mousey Mousey, Bulldozer, Peebo and Half Pint thought that Mumcat was right and they did as they were told. Mischief thought she might be wrong, and one day he wanted to see for himself.

"I'm not scared," he boasted. "I can look after myself. See you later, scaredy-cats." And off he trotted, tail in the air, into the woods behind the house, doing what Mumcat had said not to.

It was very quiet under the trees, and as Mischief trotted in a bit further, the woods grew darker and darker. The sound of a twig breaking made him jump – OOOH! The sound of the branches rustling gave him the collywobbles – AAAH! The sound of a dog barking made his fur stand up on end – EEEK!

"I'm not scared," Mischief said to himself nervously. "There's nothing to be scared of."

Then – SQUAWK!

"What was that?" he squeaked.

And – SCREECH!

"What was that?" he squealed.

And – HOOT, HOOT!

"What was that?" he shrieked.

Mischief didn't wait to find out. He ran

and he ran and he ran.
He ran to the right, he
ran to the left, he ran
straight ahead, he didn't
know where, he didn't
care where.

When at last he stopped
running, Mischief wasn't
anywhere he had ever
been before, and he didn't
know how to get back
to his Mumcat.

"I'm not scared!" he said out loud, but his tummy told him that he was.

"I'm not lost!" he said boldly, but his head told him that he was.

"That's not a fox I can see," he said anxiously, but he knew that it was.

It was a fox and it was watching him. It was a fox and it was coming after him.

Mischief

Mischief ran and he ran and he ran. He ran to the left, he ran to the right, he ran straight ahead, he didn't know where, he didn't care where.

Then, all of a sudden, he heard a voice calling, "Mischief, where are you?" and "Come back, Mischief!" and "Mischief, it's supper time." And as the woods disappeared behind him Mischief saw Featherbrain, Yum Yum, Mousey Mousey, Bulldozer, Peebo and Half Pint, all waiting for him in the garden.

"What's it like in there?" asked Peebo.

"Were you scared?" asked Bulldozer.

"Not really," said Mischief.

"Did you get lost?" asked Featherbrain.

"Not really," said Mischief.

"Did you see a fox?" asked Mousey Mousey.

"Mumcat was right, I was frightened. I got lost, and there's a fox in there," said Mischief . "Where's Mumcat? I want my Mumcat."

Then he spied her, sitting on the step, and he ran and he ran and he ran to her. He snuggled up close until he could hear her gentle purr and feel her safe tongue licking his fright away.

Mischief never went into the woods behind the house again, not until he was much older.

Half Pint

Mumcat had been given a big bowl of milk, but Mumcat was fast asleep. Half Pint saw it and wondered what it was.

"Is it for washing in?" he wondered.

"Is it for playing with?" he wondered.

"Is it for eating?" he wondered.

Half Pint

He hoped it was for eating. Whenever his brothers and sisters were around they always pushed him out of the way at food time. Now they were outside and he could have it all for himself.

Half Pint walked round the bowl and looked at the milk, then he walked round the other way and looked at it again. It was white, it was shiny, and it had a funny sort of smell.

Kitten Tales

"Is that an MMM! delicious smell, or an UGH! horrible smell?" wondered Half Pint. Then he wondered what it felt like. He stretched out a paw – ever so slowly – and dipped it in the milk. The milk was cold and wet. He pulled his paw out quickly and shook it in surprise. Drops of milk flew round the room.

Half Pint

Half Pint sat and thought for a moment, then walked round the bowl again. He would try from the other side. He stretched out his other paw – ever so slowly – then dipped it in the milk and pulled it out again. More drops of milk flew round the room as Featherbrain ran in.

"What's that?" he asked.

"I don't know," said Half Pint. "It's white and it's shiny and it's got a funny sort of smell, and when I put my paw in it feels cold and wet."

"I know what it is," said Featherbrain. "It's for washing your feet. Watch this."

He jumped his front paws straight into the bowl and his back paws followed behind. Milk spilled over the edge and lay in a puddle on the floor.

Half Pint

"Next you jump back out, then you lick the white stuff off," said Featherbrain.

He jumped out of the bowl, walking milk all over the floor, then sat down to wash himself clean.

"Are you sure that's what it's for?" asked Half Pint. "What does it taste like?"

"Funny," said Featherbrain.

"What tastes funny?" asked Yum Yum, who had come through the door.

"This paw wash," said Half Pint. "If you've got dirty paws, you stand in the paw wash, then when you get out you lick it all off and your paws are clean."

Yum Yum went over to the bowl of milk and lowered her nose. "It's got a funny sort of smell," she said. "I don't know whether it's an MMM! delicious smell or an UGH! horrible smell."

Then she lowered her nose a bit further until it went into the milk and she came up spluttering. She licked her lips carefully. "It tastes quite nice," she said.

She lowered her head again slowly and stuck her tongue into the milk. "MMM!" she said, as she licked a little more. And "MMM!" she said, as her tongue lapped and lapped.

Half Pint

"You're not supposed to drink it," said Featherbrain. "It's for washing your paws!"

"Leave some for me," cried Half Pint. "I was here first!"

But Yum Yum was too busy enjoying her creamy feast. And by the time Mumcat had woken and told her to leave some milk for Half Pint, Yum Yum had licked the bowl clean.

"Fancy drinking a bowl full of paw wash!" said Featherbrain.

"Paw wash, my foot!" said Half Pint. "That was food, and she's eaten it all up – again. It's not fair!"

Bulldozer

Bulldozer was Mumcat's little problem. He was always getting into trouble. He never did anything on purpose. Things just seemed to happen to him.

He didn't mean to smash the vase. He was chasing his tail round and round in circles and couldn't stop himself when he knocked into the table on which the vase was standing.

Kitten Tales

"Stop playing silly games," scolded Mumcat.

Bulldozer tried, but he kept forgetting.

He didn't mean to fall in the pond. He was running after a ball when it rolled into the water. He couldn't stop himself and fell in after it. Luckily Mumcat was there to pull him out.

Bulldozer

"Stop running everywhere," said Mumcat. Bulldozer tried, but he kept forgetting.

He didn't mean to knock over the cup of tea, but Mumcat said he shouldn't have been on the table.

He didn't mean to tear the curtains, but Mumcat said he shouldn't have been climbing up them.

He didn't mean to spill soap powder all over the floor, but Mumcat said if he hadn't been on top of the washing machine it wouldn't have happened. He certainly didn't mean to be shut in the boot of the car, in the dark, and taken away from home.

Mumcat had told her kittens to keep away from cars. "Cars are dangerous," she said. "Cars are noisy. Cars can run cats over. Cars and cats are not friends." But Bulldozer couldn't help jumping up to look inside the car boot when someone left it open.

Bulldozer couldn't help finding the blanket at the back. It was so very soft and comfortable. And Bulldozer couldn't help just pawing it a bit and closing his eyes, when – everything went dark.

Then BRRMM, BRRMMM! That was the noise of the car starting. And, CRUNCH, CRUNCH! That was the noise of the car wheels on the gravel. The car was *moving*!

Bulldozer sat in the dark on the blanket and shivered with fear. "I want my Mumcat," he meowed, but nobody heard him. "Let me out!" he meowed, but nobody heard him. The car went faster and faster. Every time it went round a corner, Bulldozer was thrown from side to side. What was happening? Where was he going? Where was Mumcat?

It was a long time before the car stopped. Bulldozer sat up and meowed loudly. Surely someone would hear him. Surely someone would open the boot and find him. Surely someone would take him home to Mumcat.

Bulldozer

But nobody came and soon the car started up again. Bulldozer wanted to be let out so much that he meowed the loudest MEOW! he had ever meowed in his life. And then he did it again, and again. "MEEEOOOOWWWW!"

Suddenly the boot opened and daylight streamed in. Bulldozer sat there blinking, his eyes blinded by the bright light. Then he saw a face that he recognised looking down at him in astonishment. "Am I a long way from home?" he wondered.

Kitten Tales

Bulldozer jumped up on to the side of the boot, and there he saw a house and a garden that looked just like home. Playing in the garden he saw two kittens who looked just like Mischief and Peebo, and walking towards him with her tail in the air was Mumcat!

"I'm home!" meowed Bulldozer. "I'm home!"

Bulldozer

He jumped down from the car and ran to Mumcat, purring loudly.

Mumcat licked the worry from his face. "You're a very silly kitten," she said gently. "When will you learn to do as I say?"

Bulldozer said he would try very hard. And that's just what he did, but he never stopped being Mumcat's little trouble.

Yum Yum

Yum Yum was always hungry. Even when her little round tum looked full to bursting, she would still say she was hungry. Even though she was *always* first in line when the food was dished out, and even though she *always* managed to eat just a bit more than all her brothers and sisters, she was still *always* hungry.

Yum Yum

One day when Yum Yum was in the
kitchen looking for any tasty bits that might
have fallen under the table, she heard a
strange new sound.

BUZZZ! A fly
flew through the door.

BUZZZ! The fly
flew across the room.

BUZZZ! The fly
flew back again and
hit the window.

PRRRR!
Yum Yum saw the fly.

She leapt up onto
the back of the chair.

ZZZZ! The fly
buzzed round and
round the window.

Yum Yum's
head went
round and round
after it.
Yum Yum's
bottom wriggled
ready to pounce.
Yum Yum's paws
thumped on the
window.
The fly flew off.
Yum Yum fell down.
"MEOW!" yelled
Yum Yum.
"I'll catch you next time."

The fly flew back again. ZZZZ!

Yum Yum leapt on to the chair. Paws ready, bottom ready, head ready – Yum Yum jumped. Her nose hit the window – BANG! – but never mind the OUCH! Underneath her paw on the window sill something tickled. Underneath her paw there was a quiet zzzz!

Yum Yum looked. The fly sat still. Yum Yum sniffed, and lifted her paw, just a little.

The fly fell off the window sill. Yum Yum jumped down on to the floor and looked behind the chair. Just as she did, the fly flew out past her ear and back on to the window. ZZZZ!

"Bother!" said Yum Yum.

She jumped back on to the chair, but when she got to the window the fly had gone. Gone where? Yum Yum couldn't see it and she couldn't hear a ZZZZ! The fly had disappeared.

Yum Yum

"Bother!" said Yum Yum. "All that running about and no little snack at the end of it. Now I'm *really* hungry."

Just then she heard a familiar sound. Was it a tin being opened? Was it for her? Was it teatime already? The banging of a fork on a bowl told her it was, and Yum Yum rushed into the kitchen to be first to

start eating. She was about to take a bite when – ZZZZ! – the fly landed on her bowl of food.

"*Cheek*!" meowed Yum Yum. "Buzz off! You're not eating my tea!"

She batted the fly with her paw and it flew away. But Yum Yum didn't chase it this time. She had her tea now and she wasn't going to let her brothers and sisters push in front of her. She'd think about another little snack later.

Featherbrain

Featherbrain had birds on the brain. Ever since Mumcat had told him about birds, he couldn't help thinking about them. He couldn't help watching them. And he couldn't help chasing them. The birds on the bird table were there to be caught and Featherbrain wanted to do the catching.

But he had tried, oh how he had tried! Each time he had missed, and there were all the birds – TWEET TWEET TWEET! – as though they were laughing at him.

Featherbrain's biggest problem was that when he became excited he purred loudly– PURR PURR PURR! Birds made him excited. So as soon as he was close to them, the birds could hear him purring and flew away. That meant it was no good creeping through the grass. It was no good padding softly up the steps. It was no good sitting under the bushes and waiting for hours. His purr gave him away every time – PURR PURR PURR!

Featherbrain was fed up, but the more the birds tweeted at him, the more he was determined to catch one. He would show them! So he thought up a plan.

The bird table was quite close to the house. There was a low roof he could climb on to from a bedroom window. He could wait there without being seen by the birds, and he would be too far away for them to hear him purring. As soon as there were lots of birds on the table, he would leap down and catch one of them.

"Simple!" said Featherbrain to himself, pleased with his plan.

But it wasn't as simple as he thought. The first time he tried it, the bird table fell over, and the birds all flew away – TWEET TWEET TWEET!

The second time, he was just about to leap when Yum Yum and Bulldozer ran into the garden. Bulldozer knocked into the bird table and frightened the birds away.

Third time lucky. Featherbrain waited and waited and waited. He crouched at the edge of the roof – PURR PURR PURR! He waggled his bottom, crept his front paws forward, then he was off, up into the air, down on to the table, mouth open wide, "I've got one, I've got one!"

He was just about to run off to show Mumcat when a large hand caught him round the neck, a loud voice shouted, "DROP IT, YOU NAUGHTY CAT!" and another large hand spanked his bottom.

Featherbrain let go with a yowl. Oh, the indignity of it! Oh, the unfairness of it! Oh, the disappointment of it!

And there they all were, those insufferable birds – TWEET TWEET TWEET! – laughing at him yet again. POOH! One day he would show them.

Peebo

One day Peebo met a mirror. It was the first mirror she had ever met. She didn't know it was a mirror. She thought it was another kitten.

Kitten Tales

"That's not Featherbrain, and it's not Yum Yum, and it's not Mousey Mousey, and it's not Bulldozer, and it's not Mischief, and it's not Half Pint, and it's definitely not Mumcat. So who is it?"

Peebo decided to chase the other kitten away. She crept slowly towards it. The other kitten crept towards her. She stopped and the other kitten stopped too. She squatted down and made ready to pounce. So did the other kitten.

Then Peebo pounced.

Her nose banged on something hard.
Her paws slid on something slippery. She
stepped back, sat down and shook her head.
The other kitten was still there, shaking its
head as well.

Peebo looked puzzled. "Meow," she
thought. "That kitten's got a very hard nose
and very slippery paws."

She decided to creep up again very slowly and pat the kitten gently. She squatted and waggled her bottom. The other kitten waggled its bottom too. Peebo crept forward, one paw at a time. So did the other kitten. She reached out a paw to pat the other kitten. The other kitten reached out a paw too, and they touched.

But it wasn't a soft paw that Peebo touched, it wasn't a warm paw and it wasn't a scratchy paw. It was a cold paw, a hard paw, a very strange paw indeed.

Peebo stared at the other kitten. The other kitten stared back. Peebo meowed at the other kitten. The other kitten meowed back at exactly the same time.

Kitten Tales

Now Peebo was tired.

She had played and played with her little kitten friend. She curled up in a ball and settled down to sleep. Her little kitten friend snuggled down beside her.

When Featherbrain came by, he saw Peebo asleep, and he saw another kitten just like her asleep beside her. Then he saw a kitten he hadn't seen before. It wasn't Yum Yum, and it wasn't Mousey Mousey, and it wasn't Bulldozer, and it wasn't Mischief, and it wasn't Half Pint, and it certainly wasn't Mumcat.

Featherbrain crept slowly towards the strange kitten. The kitten crept towards him. Featherbrain stopped and the other kitten stopped too. Featherbrain leapt at the other kitten. He leapt fast and hard and he banged noses with the other kitten, who leapt at the same time.

The OUCH! was too much for Featherbrain. He ran off howling and never did find out who the other kitten was. If he had looked back, he would have seen that the other kitten ran off howling too.

Mousey Mousey

Mousey Mousey caught her first mouse.

"Meow!" she exclaimed, because she was very pleased.

The mouse dropped out of her mouth and ran away.

Mousey Mousey

"Meow," cried Mousey Mousey, because she was disappointed.

Mousey Mousey caught another mouse. This time she didn't meow. She wanted to keep the mouse to show her brothers and sisters. But the mouse had other ideas. It wriggled and it squiggled and it squirmed, until it fell to the ground and ran away.

"Meow," growled Mousey Mousey, because she was cross.

Mousey Mousey caught a third mouse.

She didn't
meow, and
when the mouse
began to wriggle
and squiggle and
squirm, she held on
tight. It was Mumcat's
birthday and Mousey
Mousey wanted the mouse
for her present.
     Mousey Mousey ran indoors,
holding on tight with her teeth.
She ran upstairs, still holding on tight.

Mousey Mousey

She ran into the bedroom, where Mumcat often slept, still holding on tight.

Mumcat was in her usual place, asleep on the carpet in the corner of the bedroom. Mousey Mousey dropped the mouse by Mumcat's paws and nudged Mumcat awake. The mouse stood still.

"Happy birthday, Mumcat!" said Mousey Mousey.

"Thank you, Mousey Mousey," said Mumcat.

The mouse ran away.

"Meow!" cried Mousey Mousey. "That was your birthday present."

"Never mind," said Mumcat. "It's the thought that counts."

Mousey Mousey

Mousey Mousey was very tired from chasing mice. She put two paws on Mumcat's tum, and kneaded her gently. She put two more paws on Mumcat's tum and began to purr. "I'll catch another mouse in the morning," she said.

"Thank you," said Mumcat. "I'll look forward to that. Sleep tight, my little Mousey Mousey!"

But Mousey Mousey was already fast asleep.

Snow Monster

One winter morning when the kittens had filled their tums with breakfast, Peebo stuck her nose through the cat flap to see what she could see. What she saw made her gasp. "The garden's gone away!" she cried.

Snow Monster

"Let *me* see," said Featherbrain. He pushed Peebo out of the way. "Where's it gone away to?"

"I want to see," said Yum Yum. She pushed Featherbrain out of the way. "There's white stuff flying around. It might be something to eat. I'm going to catch some and try it."

With that she leapt through the cat flap – BANG! CRASH! WALLOP! – and disappeared in a heap of snow. Featherbrain stuck his nose out to see what she was doing and couldn't see her anywhere. "The white stuff's eaten the garden and now it's eaten Yum Yum!" he meowed to the others.

A muffled noise came from the heap of snow and Yum Yum's head popped up.

"Here I am," she said. "This white stuff is very funny," she said. "When you eat it, it's cold and wet but it's like eating nothing. Come and try some."

Mischief didn't need to be asked twice. He hurled himself through the cat flap, leapt into the air and tried to catch some white stuff.

Featherbrain, Mousey Mousey, Bulldozer, Peebo and Half Pint jumped through the cat flap to join the other two kittens. Bulldozer landed on an icy patch.

He skidded into the milk bottles and knocked them all over. Mousey Mousey played cat and mouse with the white stuff. She pounced on it, but whenever she caught a bit there was nothing there. Half Pint was so small he had to bounce like a kangaroo just to get up the path. Peebo quickly scrambled up a tree to see what she could see.

What she saw was – a *monster*!

The monster was big. The monster was fat. The monster had a long pink tongue. The monster looked frightening. AND THE MONSTER WAS WALKING TOWARDS THE OTHER KITTENS!

"Rrrrufff," ruffed the monster.
"RRRUFFF, RRRRRUFFFF."
"MEEEOOOOWWWW!" cried
Peebo. "Look out! There's a monster!"
The kittens stopped in their tracks.
They looked and they saw the big fat
monster with smoke coming out of his
mouth creeping towards them.

Featherbrain, Yum Yum, Mousey Mousey, Bulldozer and Mischief bounded quickly through the snow and leapt through the cat flap to the safety of Mumcat.

But Half Pint couldn't. With every little jump he landed in another snowy hole and his legs were so short that he just couldn't climb out.

The monster was getting closer. And closer. And closer!

"Hurry, Half Pint," squealed Peebo
from her tree. "It's catching up on you."

Half Pint leapt again and fell into more
snow. He was so tired that his legs could
hardly lift him.

The monster's nose was stretching
towards Half Pint. Smoke from his mouth
swirled around. His pink tongue hung
down hungrily.

"Look out!" yelled Peebo.

As she yelled, a great pile of snow slid from the branch with a rush and landed on the monster's head.

"HOOWWWL!" yelped the monster. It leapt into the air, sending snow flying in all directions, and hurtled off out of the garden.

Half Pint stood in his snowy hole and looked astonished. Peebo stood on her waving branch and looked amazed. Mumcat shot through the cat flap to save her little ones. She gently picked up Half Pint by the loose skin at the back of his neck and carried him back to the house. Then she came back for Peebo, who climbed down from her tree and ran back in with Mumcat, chattering all the way.

Snow Monster

When they were all safely snuggled up indoors, Mumcat told them about Dog. Dog was big, Dog was fat, Dog had a long pink tongue, Dog was frightening. But Dog was sometimes frightened too. They had frightened Dog off this time, but they must be very, very careful in future until they were big enough to look after themselves.

Christmas Kittens

Something strange was happening in the house. Things were being moved. The kittens' bed was moved from the kitchen into the hall. The kittens' bowls were moved from the kitchen to just outside the back door.

Christmas Kittens

Mumcat's favourite chair was moved into the garden shed, and that upset Mumcat a lot. Strangest of all, a tree grew in its place. *A tree! Indoors!*

Featherbrain saw it first and rushed to tell the others. "There's a tree growing in the house!" he meowed. "Come and look."

His brothers and sisters didn't believe him, but they went and looked. Featherbrain was right! There, sure enough, was a tree growing where Mumcat's chair had been.

Kitten Tales

"I'm going to climb it,"
said Mischief.
"So am I,"
said Peebo.

One after the other, seven little kittens leapt into the lower branches. The tree swayed from side to side – WHOOAH! One after the other they scrambled from branch to branch up to the very top. The tree rocked violently – WHOOAHH! – and suddenly it lurched right over – AARRGGHH! – and everything fell to the ground – CRASH!

As it fell, Bulldozer was catapulted across the room. He managed to grab a curtain and cling on. Featherbrain was thrown into the log basket. Five other furry bodies scrambled out from underneath the tree and disappeared quickly into the kitchen. They could hear someone coming.

"Bad kittens," they heard a voice say, as Featherbrain and Bulldozer were tossed in to the kitchen after the other kittens.

Five nights later, when all was quiet, Peebo saw that the door to the tree room had been left open. The kittens crept to the door to see if the tree was still there. When they looked, they couldn't believe their eyes. The tree was covered with tiny lights and brightly coloured balls and silvery bits of string which glittered and shone.

"Wow!" meowed Mischief.

"Wowee!" meowed the other kittens.

If trees were for climbing, brightly coloured balls and silvery bits of string were definitely for playing with.

Mischief rushed over and batted a big red ball with his paw. The branch of the tree bounced up and down and the ball swung from side to side.

Featherbrain bounded over and leapt in the air to pull down a long piece of silvery string. As he dragged it along the carpet, Half Pint chased it.

Mousey Mousey batted a small green ball. It fell to the ground. Mousey Mousey pretended it was a mouse and nosed it round the room, until Bulldozer jumped in, batted it hard and broke it against a table leg.

Yum Yum smelt something tasty. She sniffed and sniffed at all the shiny shapes hanging from the tree, until she sniffed one that smelt like food. She bit it and her teeth sank into delicious sweet soft brown stuff – "YUMMY, YUMMY!" She ate it up quickly and spat out the silvery wrapper, then climbed the tree to look for more.

Peebo clambered to the top of the tree and looked about her. Hanging from the ceiling there were shiny stars and colourful pieces of string. If only she could fly! Perhaps she would try!

Peebo looked at the stars and steadied herself on the top branch. She looked again and got her legs ready for take-off. She looked again and – WHEEE! – she flew from the tree and landed among the stars and strings, where she swung wildly for a few seconds before falling to the floor in a tangled heap –THUMP!

Just at that moment an extremely loud HO! HO! HO! stopped the kittens in their tracks. Another, even louder HO! HO! HO! sent them running to hide behind the tree, where they stood shaking with fright.

When they peered out, they saw a strange man with a long white beard, bright red clothes and big black boots, carrying a huge, bulging sack over his shoulder. The man stopped in front of the tree and opened the sack. Then he took out lots of gaily coloured boxes and put them under the tree. He was just putting down the last box when he heard Featherbrain purring.

"HO HO! HO! What have we got here?" said the man. He bent down and picked up Featherbrain, and when Mischief ran forward to help, he picked him up too. "Well, well, well," he said. "Christmas kittens!" When he saw ten more eyes staring at him, his "HO! HO! HO!" shook the room.

"Christmas kittens, you may be," he
said, "but should you be under the
Christmas tree?"

He gently carried the kittens out to
where Mumcat was sleeping peacefully.
They snuggled down beside her, tired from
their adventures and full of wonder at what
they had seen.

The next morning the kittens heard the crics of surprise at the mess the big man had made in the Christmas tree room. And they enjoyed the parcel of plastic mice and balls with bells and special treats that he had left under the tree. On the parcel there was a label that said, "For the Christmas kittens and their Mumcat, from Father Christmas."

Mumcat

Tortoiseshell and White

Yum Yum

Tortoiseshell and White

Bulldozer

Black with white nose

Peebo

Black and white